# Max's Daddy Goes
# to the Hospital

# Danielle Steel

# Max's Daddy Goes to the Hospital

E
STE

*Illustrated by Jacqueline Rogers*

**Delacorte
Press**

Published by
Delacorte Press
Bantam Doubleday Dell Publishing Group, Inc.
666 Fifth Avenue
New York, New York 10103

Library of Congress Cataloging in Publication Data

Steel, Danielle.
Max's Daddy goes to the hospital / by Danielle Steel ; illustrated
by Jacqueline Rogers.
p.    cm.
Summary: When his father is injured while rescuing three
children from a fire, Max is very worried about him until he is
finally allowed to visit him in the hospital.
ISBN 0-385-29797-1
[1. Fathers—Fiction. 2. Hospitals—Fiction. 3. Fire fighters—
Fiction. 4. Family life—Fiction.]  I. Rogers, Jacqueline, ill.
II. Title.
PZ7.S8143Maxm   1989
[E]—dc19                                          89-1536
                                                     CIP
                                                      AC


design by Judith Neuman-Cantor


Manufactured in the United States of America

November 1989

10 9 8 7 6 5 4 3 2 1

*To Maxx, wonderful, brave, happy,*
*cuddly, yummy little boy*
*whom we love so much and*
*who brings us so much joy.*

*Love,*
*Mommy*

This is Max. His Mommy is a nurse, and his Daddy is a fireman. He lives in New York and he is four years old.

Max loves to visit his Daddy at the
firehouse, and see the firemen. They have
ladders and fire trucks and a fireman's
pole. A big alarm sounds when the firemen
have to go to a fire. It's a little scary
sometimes when they go to a fire. They
could get hurt. What they do is dangerous,
even though they are always very careful.

Max's Mommy works at a hospital. She is a nurse and she works in the nursery. That's where they take care of new babies when they are born. Max likes to visit his Mommy and see the tiny babies.

One day, the phone rang first thing in the morning while Max's Mommy was making waffles. Max's Daddy was working at the firehouse. He had been there since the night before. Max's Mommy looked very worried when she was on the telephone. When she hung up, she sat down next to Max at the breakfast table.

"Daddy just got hurt. In a big fire at a big hotel." Her eyes looked very big to Max. Max was worried too. He loved his Daddy very much. He didn't want anything to happen to him.

"Did he get burned?" Max's eyes were big and frightened.

"No," his Mommy said quietly, "he broke his leg and his arm. But he saved two little girls and a baby."

"Wow!" Max was very proud of his
Daddy, but he was worried too. "Will he
be all right?"

"Yes, he will. But he'll have to stay in
the hospital for a few days," his Mommy
said.

"Can I visit him?"

"I think so. I'm going to visit him right
after I drop you off at school. I'll tell
you if you can see him when I pick you
up at Jean's this afternoon." Jean was
Max's baby-sitter.

Max's Mommy cleaned up the breakfast dishes. Then she put on her nurse's uniform. It was lucky that Max's Daddy had been taken to the same hospital where Max's Mommy worked. Max and his Mommy were very quiet on the way to school that morning. They were both thinking about Max's Daddy.

Max's Mommy kissed him good-bye.
And then she left to go to the
hospital to see Daddy.

Max's baby-sitter Jean picked him up at school that afternoon. Max told her all about how his Daddy rescued two little girls and a baby from a fire in a hotel. And how he had broken a leg and an arm and was in the hospital.

"I know," Jean said calmly. "Your Mommy called this morning. She said that your Daddy is feeling much better."

"Can I see him?"

"I don't know," Jean said. "Your Mommy will tell you all about that when she picks you up this afternoon."

But when his Mommy picked him up
at Jean's, she said his father was sleeping.
He was too tired to have any visitors
yet, not even Max. And Max was very
disappointed.

"But can't I see him anyway? I can
watch him sleep."

"Wouldn't you rather see him tomorrow,
when he's feeling better?"

"No!" There were tears in Max's eyes.
He was angry and sad that he couldn't
go to the hospital to see his Daddy. He
argued with his Mommy about it all the
way home. She still said Max had to wait
until the next day to see his Daddy.

When Max's Mommy was cooking
dinner that night, they saw his Daddy on
TV. The man on the news said that
Max's Daddy was a hero because he had
saved the two little girls and the baby.
Max was so proud of him!

But later that night, Max was worried about his Daddy. Why wouldn't his Mommy let him see him? Maybe he was sicker than she said. Maybe he had more than just a broken arm and leg. And what if something really terrible happened to him? All kinds of scary thoughts ran around in Max's head. Finally he fell asleep.

In the morning when he woke up,
Max felt a little better.

He felt much better when his Daddy
called him. His Daddy said he felt a lot
better and he wanted to see Max after
school.

That day, Max could hardly sit still in
school. All he wanted was for the day
to be over so he could visit his Daddy.

Finally, his Mommy came to take him to see his Daddy. On the way they bought flowers and some balloons. When they got to the hospital, they rode up in the elevator. Max had been in it before, when he visited his Mommy in the nursery with the new babies.

The elevator stopped on the fourth floor. They walked down a long corridor. Max's Mommy stopped at a door, and then opened it for Max to go in.

Max walked in slowly, holding the flowers and the balloons. There in the bed was his Daddy.

The bed had a bar over the top, and a little triangle for Max's Daddy to hang on to. It helped him move around on the bed. His leg was in a big cast propped up on pillows, and so was his arm. There was a tube in his other arm attached to a bag of water. His Mommy said that was called an "IV." It was just like water going into Daddy's arm, and Daddy didn't feel it. Max's Daddy smiled the biggest smile in the world when he saw Max and his Mommy.

For a minute, Max was a little scared by the bed and the casts on his Daddy's arm and leg, and the IV tube in his arm. It all looked a little scary. But it still looked like Daddy lying on the bed. Max sure was happy to see him.

    His Daddy pushed a button and
lowered his bed. He invited Max to hop
onto it next to him.

    "I'll show you how the bed works." He
smiled. "Seeing you makes me feel
better." Max hopped on the bed and
cuddled up next to his Daddy. He
showed Max the button that made the

back of the bed go up like a chair.
Another button made the foot of the bed
go up. Max's Daddy then made the
whole bed go up and down, like an
airplane lifting off the ground. Max
pushed all the buttons too. The bed
bumped way up and it felt like they
could almost touch the ceiling. His Daddy
let him work the television too. Finally
Max's Mommy said they had to let Daddy
rest, or he'd be too tired to come home
the next morning. Max felt much better
when he kissed his Daddy good-bye
because he knew he was all right now.

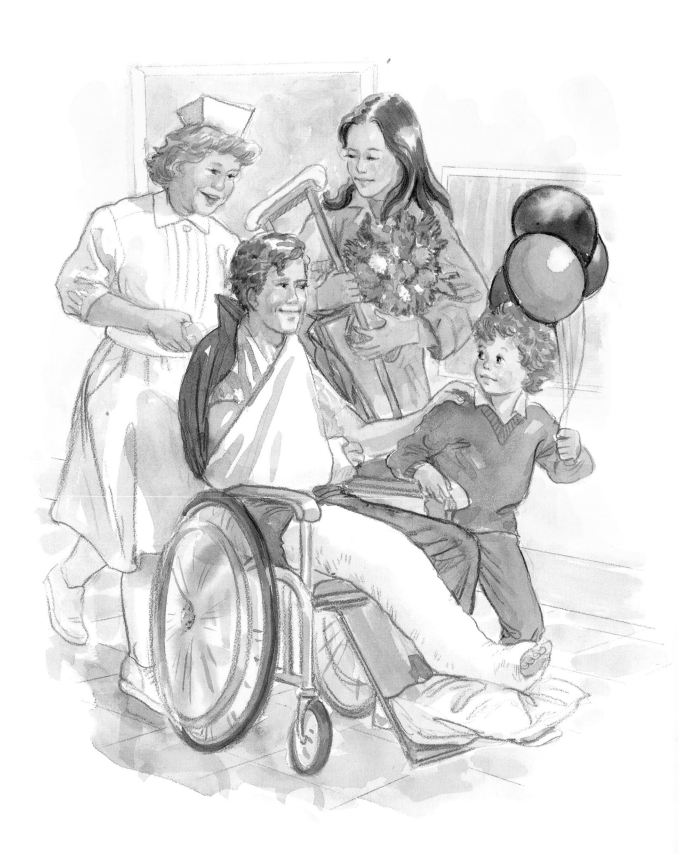

The next day was Saturday. Max and his Mommy went to the hospital to bring his Daddy home. A nurse pushed him in a wheelchair until they reached the car. Then she helped him get in. He could use only one crutch because of his broken arm. He groaned when he got in the car because it hurt him. But right after that, he smiled at Max and said everything was okay and not to worry. He kissed Max's Mommy. She told him she loved him. She started the car and drove them home and helped Daddy inside. He still had the cast on his leg and the one on his arm. But he didn't have the IV tube in his arm anymore because he was already a lot better.

Max's Mommy put his Daddy to bed.
She propped his leg up on pillows and
told him to rest while she made lunch.
Max climbed into bed with his Daddy so
he wouldn't be lonely. Max had made
two get-well cards and a big sign that
said "Welcome home! We love you,
Daddy." It had flowers and rainbows in
the corners.

Max's Mommy brought in a delicious
lunch of all Daddy's favorite things:
homemade mushroom soup and spaghetti

and meatballs and chocolate chip cookies and chocolate ice cream.

Max's Daddy stayed home from the firehouse for the next six weeks while he got better. It was wonderful for Max having him at home so much, but it was hard, too, because some of the time his Daddy didn't feel so good. When his leg hurt him too much, sometimes he got grumpy. It made Max sad, too, to see his Daddy walking with a cast and a crutch, when they both wanted to be out playing baseball.

But soon they were playing baseball again. The cast and crutch were gone. Max's Daddy went back to the firehouse again. He was as good as new, and his leg and his arm didn't even hurt him.

A week later, after Max's Daddy went back to work, there was a special ceremony for him. The fire chief gave Max's Daddy a medal for bravery for saving the two little girls and the baby in the hotel fire. Max and his Mommy were very proud of Max's Daddy for being so brave.

But they were even happier because
he was all well now.